AF522418

DIWAN OF INAYAT KHAN

عنایت خان

Blessings
Inayat Khan

[illegible]

DIWAN OF INAYAT KHAN

Rendered into Verse by
JESSIE DUNCAN WESTBROOK

Sufism is the Religious Philosophy of
Love, Harmony and Beauty

MOTILAL BANARSIDASS PUBLISHERS
PRIVATE LIMITED • DELHI

First Indian Edition: 1996

ISBN: 81-208-1429-0 (Cloth)
ISBN: 81-208-1430-4 (Paper)

Also available at:

MOTILAL BANARSIDASS
41 U.A. Bungalow Road, Jawahar Nagar, Delhi 110 007
8, Mahalaxmi Chamber, Warden Road, Mumbai 400 026
120 Royapettah High Road, Mylapore, Madras 600 004
Sanas Plaza, Subhash Nagar, Pune 411 002
16 St. Mark's Road, Bangalore 560 001
8 Camac Street, Calcutta 700 017
Ashok Rajpath, Patna 800 004
Chowk, Varanasi 221 001

PRINTED IN INDIA
BY JAINENDRA PRAKASH JAIN AT SHRI JAINENDRA PRESS,
A-45 NARAINA, PHASE I, NEW DELHI 110 028
AND PUBLISHED BY NARENDRA PRAKASH JAIN FOR
MOTILAL BANARSIDASS PUBLISHERS PRIVATE LIMITED,
BUNGALOW ROAD, DELHI 110 007

FOREWORD.

THIS little garland of Sufi Songs is the expression of some of the different aspects of Sufic thought and feeling. Sufism is the Super-religion, that which contains the essence of all religions. It uses the phraseology of the country and race to which the Sufi belongs. Thus, though the Sufi is traditionally known as the mystic of Islam, because the most important Sufi poets have been of Arabia, Persia, and of the Muslim community of India, yet the Sufi would acknowledge as of his confraternity the Hebrew Prophets, the Buddhist and Brahman Seers, the mystic Saints of Christianity. He is constantly in revolt against the priesthood of an organised religion, and denies that salvation or mukti or najat can be attained through forms and ceremonies; for his is that religion of bhakti or love which in every country appears as the fine flower expressing the soul of all creeds. He regards asceticism as unnecessary, holding the loves of earth as symbols and even as parts of the Divine Love. The great Self of the Universe is to be found within the human heart, and the task of the Sufi is to perceive that his own soul is identical with the Universal Soul. When the illusion of separateness, which is the cause of all trouble and pain, disappears, the soul, awaking from the dream of life, will know itself one with God.

Some of these verses are didactic—the spiritual teacher exhorting his disciple; some are traditional symbolic tales. Some are the Sufi's efforts to interpret earthly life and its relations as shadows and emblems of the life of the soul. And, as the writer is a musician, in these Songs we hear the voice of the singer who seeks through ecstasy to obtain Divine Wisdom.

J. D. W.

CONTENTS.

To my Murshid.

O MURSHID, blessed light by Allah given
To be my Friend, my Counsellor, my Guide,
By thee in admiration and in love
My life's supreme desire is satisfied.

Within the sacred path of Sufic lore
My steps were set ; I drank the enchanted wine,
My soul was filled with light, my heart with love,
My humble body Allah's holy shrine.

Upon thy worshipped feet I laid mine eyes,
And from mine inner sight was drawn the veil ;
Captain thou wert of sacred Wisdom's ship,
Upon the sea of love we set our sail.

Thy Mureed cares not if he sink or swim
Within the crystal currents of Love's sea,
For Death and Life are one, and he would drink
Poison for nectar with felicity.

If fair within the Heaven of Heavens thou shine,
Happy were I thy cherished face to see ;
But if thou dwell within the deepest hell,
So thou were there, then it were heaven to me.

If God Himself with welcoming words of love
To me His sheltering arms should open wide,
And thou, with sin o'er-burdened, looked at me,
Then would I hasten gladly to thy side.

I ask no miracle to prove thee saint ;
I know not, I, by love and rapture taught,
Thy knowledge nor thy virtue to compute,
My faith for barren Reason careth naught.

The scoffing world may jeer at me in vain,
And hold my simple holy faith as blind,
But in this blindness, willing, open-eyed,
A secret, intimate, earnest joy I find.

No more am I alone, not separate
From thee am I, but thou art one with me,
My soul hath called thee Master, my Murshid,
And fixed its faith unshakeably on thee.

Nor judge I now henceforth the good nor ill,
Nor weigh within my mind the right, the wrong,
But bending o'er my Vina do I breathe
My deep devotion in impassioned song.

One with the mighty Universe am I,
Within each being hath my soul its part,
I weep ecstatic tears of joy, and sigh,
The thought of thee o'erflows my grateful heart.

And as my tears fall down in happy showers
They turn to pearls in silver hue that gleam,
And wreathing sighs that rise from out my heart
The lovely forms of heavenly Houris seem.

Some say that Love enslaves the lover's heart,
That bonds, and chains, and prison-bars it gives,
But Love the Liberator I declare,
None but the lover free, unfettered lives.

Love that is bought and sold is naught to me,
Far other the devotion I present,
Selfless and humble shall the longing be
Wherewith my seeking soul shall be content.

O let me speak with lowliness thy name,
Muhammad Abu Hashim Mudani,
Immortal in thy splendour ; thy Mureed
His dream, his inspiration draws from thee.

O Pir-o-Murshid, ne'er shall I forget
The true words of the teaching thou dost speak
All ill came from my yet unworthy self,
All good from thy inayat which I seek.

Saki.

GIVE me a cup, O Saki, of thy Wine
Rose-red and sparkling; with thy voice divine
Sing me the Song of Life. O, from thy face
Uplift the veil, that I may see thy grace,
Thy lips of ruby-red that I may kiss,
And, swooning in the ocean of my bliss,
Forget that thou and I are separate.
Life's sorrow I lay by,—the desolate,
The weary pain of life exists for me
No more, the dark and dread anxiety
That all the sorrow of to-morrow fears
Is cast away; no sighs, no bitter tears,
No dull forebodings more. In ecstasy
Of love my soul, O Saki, turns to thee.
O love me now! I only ask thy smile
To gild this life that lasts a little while.
Unloose thy hair, unplait each golden tress,
Let my heart bathe within its loveliness.
Here is my life—what is my life to me?
I offer it a sacrifice to thee,
So may I see thy beauty all divine.

I broke the jar, O Saki, spilt the Wine;
Forgive my heart with pain and shame afire
I have cut down the plant of my desire
That I unto thy will may be resigned.
My love has fettered me and made me blind.
Thy Wine has caught and borne my spirit up,
Till, in the circle of thy shining cup,

I see the world and all the planets move,
The sun, the stars, the moon, in spheres of love;
Life falls and rises in unceasing waves,
Thy Wine is all my thirsty spirit craves.

When I, uplifted, on my Vina play,
Over my head the perfumed roses sway,
And Saki sings his love in endless tale
While sweet above us trills the nightingale.

O Saki-I-Alishan, thou couldst bring
Heaven upon earth if thou my songs would sing.
In exaltation all have I forgot,
My name, my fame shall I remember not;
I veil them both to let thy glory shine.
I have abandoned all that once was mine,—
My friends, my foes, mine earthly joys and cares
Are naught to me, whose eager foot-fall fares
Upon the road that leads unto thy door.
My Friend and my Belovéd—even more
My God art thou! Though Death and bitter Fate
Have left me broken and unfortunate,
Haunting my path since I have loved thy face,
My hallowed heart is still thy dwelling-place.

The Sufi.

FORMLESS, unlimited the Sufi's Allah,
  The Soul of all—the all in all that lives,
And Nature is Muhammad, his Inspirer;
  Each new experience the new day gives,
A Sura of Korán. Wisdom alone
  He takes as teacher of the lore divine,
His body is the Mosque, his Rosary
  The rhythmic breath, the holy Kaaba Shrine
Is built within the Sufi's secret heart;
  His Najat is the earthly body's death;
His Islam is the brotherhood of man;
  Muslim—who knoweth truth and followeth;
His Prayer he offers to the Self within;
  Kafír is he who wandereth aside;
Jennat within himself the Sufi makes,
  Dozakh by which his heart is purified.
He mourns not o'er the future nor the past,
  To-day alone is precious in his sight
Wherein to live and act; he waiteth not
  To-morrow's call, but lives each day aright;
Each day of life to him is Judgment Day;
  This earthly world is Hell unto his eyes;
His life is but a pilgrimage to Heaven;
  The Life Beyond his aim, his goal, his prize.
His virtue is to keep in his own sight
  His conscience clean and fair, his only sin
To live in darkness knowing not his soul,
  Ignorant of the Self that dwells within.

And Satan is the Ego dark and dull;
  Rahman to him the glad awakened mind;
Drinking the Wine of Love in ecstasy
  His rapture, his enchantment shall he find.

Before him like the fair Belovéd's face
  His far ideal shines: his love is bliss;
And both the worlds are the Belovéd's lips
  Whereon his contemplation is the kiss.
The Sufi holds that he himself is all,
  God's high and mystic Name his mystery,
To live in love and wisdom is his creed;
        To lift the veil
                that parteth Thee from Me.

Oneness of Allah.

ALLAH is ONE Alone!
Look on the Universe and find the proof ;
Within the House of Life are many rooms,
Above them all the one o'er-sheltering Roof.

And round the unit One
All numbers circle if ye reckon clear,
To add or to divide, the great, the small,
One as the centre symbol doth appear.

Within the world of men
Allah hath shown His oneness in each face ;
For each is different, and is unique
In all the changing crowds that make our race.

And not in man alone :
The earth is earth in ever-varying guise,
The rocks, the trees, and even man himself
Are dust, as that which 'neath his footstep lies.

And water too is one,
The rivers wild, the gentle streams that glide,
The quiet lake, the kindly drops of rain,
Are one with ocean's never-resting tide.

And light and fire are one ;
The sun that rules the day, the moon by night,
The wild volcano, and the electric spark
That tamed can yield our homes its kindly light.

The gentle air we breathe,
That bubbles in the water, can arise
And, passing through the earth, can wed with fire,
To form the ether round the air that lies.

From ether come they all,
The primal elements that four we name
And know as individual, yet they pass
Returning to the ether whence they came.

Some can no deeper see
Than Nature, and to all beyond are blind ;
The Sufi sayeth, " Allah ho Akbar "—
The All-in-All, Within, Beyond, Behind.

Some worship many gods,
And some, denying, bow the knee to none ;
By divers names, in many varying lands,
Men call on Thee,—but Thou art only *ONE*.

And yet to call Thee ONE
Were limiting to Thy infinity !
How can I speak to Thee as separate
Since I, as all beside, exist in Thee ?
But language follows Thee with halting feet,
And bows the knee in all humility.

The Kiss.

HIGHEST of all loves is the Love Divine.
  What is this love then that uplifts mankind?—
For Man is made after the form of God,—
  What soul, what spirit, hidden lurks behind

Who boasts to know alone the Love of God,
  And scoffs at human loves as mean and low,
Is blinded by his pride and arrogance,
  And lives despising what he may not know.

Upward through bird and beast doth love aspire
  To reach its glory in the heart of Man,
Through all the ages Nature strives and mounts
  Towards him, the culmination of her plan.

For God Himself is Love, and is expressed
  In the full rapture of the lover's bliss,
And the whole Universe is built of Love
  Whose symbol is the meeting and the kiss.

The glowing kiss of fire to ashes burns,
  The healing kiss of water purifies,
The kiss of air brings life, and growth, and strength,
  The kiss of ether can etherealize.

The steel is drawn towards the magnet's kiss,
  The rose unfolds beneath the kiss of dew,
The whole world kisses in its ecstasy,
  And joy arises and is ever new.

Kissing the mother's breast the child is fed,
  Hand kisses loving hand, in close embrace,
Form kisses form, and eyes in glances kiss,
  Cheek kisses cheek when face is held to face.

Kissing the face shows love's own tender heart,
  Kissing the brow the inspiring breath of love,
Kissing the lips love's goal and end supreme,
  Kissing the eyes the mind that soars above.

Kiss on the ear holdeth the lover fast,
  Kiss on the neck bringeth the lover near,
Kiss on the hair makes it a net for love,
  Kiss on the head driveth out lover's fear.

A kiss upon the shoulder courage gives,
  To kiss the hand means adoration free,
A kiss upon the knee shows reverence,
  To kiss the feet is deep humility.

The kiss of thought is understanding clear,
  And sympathy the heart's sincerest kiss,
Souls kiss in merging in the spirit's light,
  Conscious of God they reach the utmost bliss.

A Caravan.

FROM Ajum to Aráb, a caravan
Passed on its way; and men of many kinds,
Chance-met, discoursed of life and circumstance,
The hopes and the desires of diverse minds.

The MERCHANT said:
Money is all supreme,
Nothing the world desires or worships more,
All bow before it, fearing Poverty,
That grisly shape that lurks beside the door.

It serves the needs that haunt us day by day;
Nay more,—our joys and our delights obtains;
Men say that Allah is the Lord of all,
But I maintain that only Money reigns.

The SCHOLAR said:
My world is otherwise,
I care for Learning's lustre round my name,
For statesmanship, for letters, and for art,
For science that can yield us deathless fame.

Whose life and work is dedicate to these,
Who loves as Learning's willing slave to live,
He is the ruler of mankind, to him
The laurel crown the grateful world shall give.

Then spake the HEDONIST:
Life is so brief
And joy so fleeting; who would sacrifice
Delight for wealth or fame? Laborious days
And weary nights are all too great a price.

Be ours to feast, and drink the ruby wine,
And rest with roses strewn upon our bed,
Revel with the belovéd while we may,
And kiss the lips that now are young and red.

Then said the PRIEST:
O friends, ye walk astray
That tread not true Religion's holy path,
Who loves good action and wise thought and speech
The guiding light that leads aright he hath.

These earthly things ye cherish pass away,
As Life itself will leave you after all,
Its joys dissolving as the morning mist
Vanishing in the sun, when Death shall call.

Then woke the SUFI from his trance of bliss,
And in his eyes there lingered still the gleam,
The light from far away. The travellers paused
And listened silently unto his dream;

He said:
Though life in many-changing guise
Beguiles with right and wrong, and peace and strife,
Over it all sounds the harmonious song
That Nature sings—her holy hymn of life.

And in the Drama of the Universe
Allah has given us each, in joy and pain,
On life's tremendous stage our part to play;
The Curtain falls—only to rise again.

Mother.

NAUGHT hast thou grudged, O Mother, for thy children,
No sword of pain, no load of suffering;
Thy loving-kindness like a mantle folds us,
Thy sheltering love is all encompassing.

Thou gavest us our body for a garment
In which our souls expanded, like the flowers
Under the gardener's care ; so all we vaunt of—
Our strength, our skill, our power—are thine, not ours.

Thy heart a delicate instrument responding
To every pang thy children feel or fear ;
Their pain thy pain ; thine infant's cry of anguish
Thy listening heart attentive leaps to hear.

Thine arms are Nature's ever-ready cradle,
Thy smile on us is bliss, as from above
Thou bendest with thy kiss, our souls are lifted
With waves o'er-flowing of the sea of love.

Our childish woes found sweetest consolation
In loving sympathy that tarried long
And wearied never, and thy voice at twilight
Brought slumber on the gentle wings of song.

Thou art the Mother-Goddess visible,
No other worldly love is pure as thine,
None other free from earthly stain and passion,
Selfless and endless, wonderful, divine.

Before the gate of birth to us was opened,
How many weary days hadst thou to bear
To mould our bodies to the form of manhood!
And ever since with wise and anxious care

Thou broodest o'er thy children. Even thy presence,
Thy words, can heal the heart that sorrows much,
And calm the troubled spirit ; thou canst solace,
Canst charm and comfort with thy magic touch.

What child is happy knowing thou art grieving
Over his coldness, for he is a part
Of thee, and feels with thee, even as a flower
Must perish if decay be at its heart ?

The warmest love of brother and of sister,
Of wife, of husband, pales before thy fire,
More than a father's is thy selfless passion,
Deeper and stronger than the world's desire.

The holy Mother Mary with the Christ-Child
Bends o'er the world with benediction sweet,
And down the ages comes Muhammad's saying,
That Heaven is lying at a Mother's feet.

The Infant.

LOVE'S loveliest expression is the Babe,
Whom from the trouble of this weary age
All turn to love, and from whose presence flows
The inspiration of the Saint and Sage.

Whose sweet appeal makes Allah merciful,
Before whose light the Angels veil their eyes,
Who, guarded by the shelter of the Lord,
Brings unto earth the airs of Paradise.

For all the infant knows of life is love,
The Mother's watchfulness, the Father's care:
They, smiling at its innocent delight,
Forget the woes Earth's children have to bear.

And at each doorstep Santa Claus shall call
With loads of children's cheer and gaiety,
While for the festival of household mirth
Allah himself has reared the Christmas Tree.

The little babe, the friend of all the world,
Who knows no stranger underneath the sun
Gives readily its willing smile to all,
Regarding evil things and good as one.

It recks not if in wealth or poverty
Its way be set, in happiness or strife;
Cherished, or left neglected and forgot,
Within it springs the joyful fount of life.

The only treasure that the world can give
Its mother's milk ; it gains not any joy
From rich attire ; sweeter than music's charms
Its rattle, dear as precious gems its toy.

And thus the Sufi worships innocence
In worshipping the child, and seeks release
From earthly sorrows ; like a child to live,
Simple and unconcerned, in joy and peace.

Satan and Rahman.

RAHMAN said: In the human heart revealed
 My spirit shines, in Man made manifest;
In this abode of flesh, creation's crown,
 Is evolution's highest thought expressed,

For in mine image have I moulded Man,
 Inspired him with my breath to know and feel;
At my command before him in the dust
 Heavenly and earthly creatures humbly kneel.

But Satan said: Though all these bow the knee,
 My pride shall never in the dust be hurled:
What is this Man that I should reverence him?
 Am I not conqueror of all the world?

Rahman said: Satan, is it then enough
 To hold man through his passing years thy thrall?
For knowest thou there is another Life
 Beyond this world, its restless rise and fall?

Then Satan laughed: Who knoweth the unknown,
 Or whether any God at all there be?
To feast, to dance, to eat and drink is mine,
 To spend life's fleeting hour in revelry.

Said Rahman: What a tyrant is the flesh,
 The body caring for the body's need!
Selfish and helpless, making life a hell,
 Desiring all its pride and lust to feed.

Then Satan laughed, and to Rahman he said:
Where dwells, unheeding and aloof, thy God?
Can virtue win thee pleasure, riches, fame?
Or goodness find gold-nuggets in the sod?

Rahman replied: Riches and fame and power
Are fleeting, and the human heart is vain
That builds its hope on these; to-day success
It knows, to-morrow disillusion's pain.

Said Satan: How fanatical the good
Unfitted in this striving world to live!
Down-trodden in the fight, the generous
Are left with nothing in their hands to give.

Rahman spoke: Now indeed thou knowest not
The joy austere that true believers find,
Treading in virtue's cold and stony path;
Thine ignorance hath made thee mad and blind.

Then answered Satan: I have many ways
To drag man's heart to ruin in the mire—
The snare of wealth, the love of fame and power,
The lure of ease, the fetters of desire.

Then Rahman owned: My followers are few,
Not many drink the streams of heavenly wine,
The Cousir's nectar, few the cherished souls
Who virtue-loving seek the way divine.

Smiled Satan saying: Why are senses given
If not for our delight? our mouth to gain
Pleasure from food, our ears to hear the chink
Of hoarded gold, our eyes to look disdain.

Our head was given to hold in battle high,
Our arms to deal destruction in the fight,
Our body for our lusts and our desires,
Our feet to dance in revel all the night.

Then said Rahman: Our eyes were given to see
In nature's grace God's beauty shining fair,
Our ears to hear the Holy Word of God,
Our lips to utter forth devoutest prayer.

The head was given to bow before the Lord,
The arm to help the world in pious deeds,
Body for toil, while holy errands move
The feet to minister to others' needs.

Said Satan: When the veil of Death shall lift,
Blank nothingness is all that will remain.
For Heaven is false and Hell an idle jest,
Nature is dead and all your dreams are vain.

Devotion is a foolish useless spell,
Religion built of legends from of old,
Philosophy an empty web of words,
And mysticism a tale by dreamers told.

Then Rahman said: The soul must live beyond
This life to carry on for good or ill
The deeds of earth, thus building Heaven and Hell;
And nature is a thing of Allah's Will.

Philosophy the wisdom is of God,
Devotion winning near by ecstasy,
Religion is the binding moral law,
And mysticism the secret intimate way.

Said Satan: Many souls have I enslaved,
I am the lord of all and sway the crowd
Of Adam's feeble race to sinful deeds,
But my unconquered head was never bowed.

But Rahman smiled and spake: Forever blind!
Celestial truth is hidden from thy sight;
The dark and shuddering souls that follow thee
Exiled from Allah's presence walk in night.

The Graveyard.

ONCE in a graveyard pondering I went
With thoughtful steps, and, looking on the road,
  I saw a naked skull,
Cast up dishonoured from its dark abode.

It spoke to me: O turn thy heedless foot,
Listen, O friend, give ear to my distress,
  And linger here awhile,
Out of compassion for my loneliness.

In days departed long, when life was mine,
Desire I had, and joy, and haughty pride,
  But now a helpless thing
I tarry, in oblivion cast aside.

Once they were mine, life's intimate delights,
The sweet familiar home, the household ways,
  The love of child and wife,
The sun-filled path serene of happy days.

But came disease, the harbinger of Death,
And Death, that earthly joys and sorrows ends
  With his black wine of sleep,
And sad farewells, and tears, and mourning friends.

Some cared but little where my soul had gone,
Some weighed my life, balanced for good or ill
  My earthly score of deeds;
Some true hearts sorrowed, unforgetting still.

Erstwhile, within the circle of my days
The eager joys of life around me whirled,
  But now I lie forgot,
While passes on the pageant of the world.

Self-Warning.

O SELF, awaken from thy slumber deep!
Death watcheth thee; thy careful vigil keep
Over thyself, nor on this life depend
Knowing not when thy hurrying days shall end.
Seest thou not how many passing on
Behind the impenetrable veil have gone?
In ignorance blind and bound by many ties
Fast to the world, when death shall call, "Arise
And come" then shalt thou keep unto the last
Thy petty poor possessions, holding fast
What was not thine, but things that pass and fade
Out of the web of vain illusion made.

When thou art happy, all will laugh with thee;
But poor, then none will share thy misery.
Thy life was spent with many a happy friend
But in thy grave their comradeship will end,
And thou forgotten as a tale long told,
While they make merry with thy treasured gold.
If thou be prospering, thou hast no foe,
Unfortunate, thy wealth and friends shall go
On the same road from thee. If wise thou be
Men call thee cunning, and they mock at thee
If thou be simple; if but once thou slip,
Not all thy virtue nor thy statesmanship
Shall wash away the stain. Men name thee fool
If thou obey, and if thou rise to rule
They call thee tyrannous. With earthly gain
Thou art content, but nothing shall remain

When earth itself hath passed. Thou didst avoid
Thy duty left forgot, whilst thou enjoyed
The slothful path of pleasure and of ease,
Enslaved by passion and its fantasies.
The more thou hadst, the more didst thou demand,
But earth can never fill thy greedy hand,
It shall absorb thine energy from thee.
All that befalls is fated and must be,
All that is born, or built by man's command
Sprung from the earth, or made by human hand,
Mortality doth follow. Ere Death smite
Look upon Allah, walk within his light.

Make thyself perfect ere thou try to teach
Thy fellow-man, and if thou cannot reach
Perfection, bear thyself in humble guise,
Know thy own faults, and be not overwise
To see thy brother's, but, restrained and meek
Think deep and ponder well ere thou dost speak.
Mysterious Self, O learn to know and see
Thyself, ere Death demand thy soul of thee.

Tansen.

TANSEN, the singer, in great Akbar's Court
Won great renown; through the Badshahi Fort
His voice rang like the sound of silver bells
And Akbar ravished heard. The story tells
How the King praised him, gave him many a gem,
Called him chief jewel in his diadem.
One day the singer sang the Song of Fire,
The Deepak Râg, and burning like a pyre
His body burst into consuming flame.
To cure his burning heart a maiden came
And sang Malhar, the song of water cold,
Till health returned, and comfort as of old.
" Mighty thy Teacher must be and divine,"
Great Akbar said, " magic indeed is thine,
Learnt at his feet." Then happy Tansen bowed
And said, " Beyond the world's ignoble crowd
Scorning its wealth remote and far-away
He dwells within a cave of Himalay."
" Could I but see him once," desired the King
" Sit at his feet awhile, and listening
Hear his celestial song, I would deny
My state and walk in robes of poverty."
Then said Tansen, " As you desire, Huzoor,
Indeed t'were better as a slave and poor
To come; for he, lifted above the things
Of earth, disdains to sing to earthly kings."

Long was the road, and Akbar as a slave
Followed Tansen who rode towards the cave
High in the mountains. At the singer's feet
They knelt and prayed with supplication sweet :—
" Towards thy shrine, lo, we have journeyed long
O Holy Master, bless us with thy song ! "
Then Ostad, won by their humility
Sang songs of peace and high felicity,
The Malkous Râga all ecstatic rang
Till birds and beasts, enchanted as he sang,
Gathered to hear. O'er Akbar's dreaming soul
He felt the waves of heavenly rapture roll,
But, as he turned to speak his words of praise
Ostad had vanished from his wondering gaze.
" Tell me, Tansen, what theme this is that holds
The soul enchanted, and the heart enfolds
In high delight ;" and, when he knew the name
" Tell me," again he said, " could you the same
Theme sing to lure my heart to paths untrod ? "
" Ah no, to thee I sing, he sings to GOD."

Ruzak.

KNOCK, and the answer is awaiting you,
Christian, or Muslim you may be, or Jew,
Of ancient lineage or of peasant breed,
For Ruzak recketh not of caste nor creed;
Friend, foe, alike by him are satisfied,
The gates of mercy stand forever wide.

In differing forms, by many a varied name,
Men know and hail him, but he is the same
In changeless essence. With wide open hands
To feed the million needs of earth he stands.
Your sustenance was ere your birth prepared,
With you her food your patient Mother shared.
Men, birds, and beasts, the tiny dancing world
That in the water and the air is whirled,
Germ, insect, fish, with all their myriad needs,
Clamorous and recurrent, Ruzak feeds.
Some lounge in ease, some eat their daily bread
Salt with the sweat of toil, yet all are fed.

Shame were it, loving Rezk, to give no thought
To Ruzak the Bestower, who hath brought
To each his portion, his allotted share.
And as the child, knowing his Mother's care,
In hunger looks to her to help and feed,
So should we call on Ruzak in our need.

The Nargis.

ONCE in the Place of Tombs
I, wandering deep in meditation, found
A shining Nargis plant,
Whose flowers, like eyes, looked from the dusty ground.

And, marvelling, I said,
" Why flourish here, O Flower, so shy and fair,
When even in Gulistan
Or Bostan's groves thou art remote and rare ? "

It spoke, " I am no flower ;
Behold me, saddened and disconsolate,
I am a lover's eye,
That watches and that weeps its bitter fate.

In foolish faith I held
The promise of my Heart's-Belovéd true,
And now I wait, past hope,
Past death itself, with love that springs anew.

My heart became a harp,
And Memory's fingers on its chords can play,
My Kismet is to wait
Through the long ages till the Judgment Day.

And now my spirit knows
Love is immortal, and hath given to me,
As to all lovers true,
A share of his own immortality."

Kismet.

BEFORE our births, Kussam who makes our fate
Ordained us happy or unfortunate,
And wrote upon our brow and on our hands
The signs that tell to him who understands
Our Destiny, decreed for good or ill.
So pass the Wise, bending to Allah's will,
Their lives into His mighty hands resigned.

One child is cherished; one to hands unkind
Is given; one dies in life's first shining dawn;
One longs to die, but Death when called upon
Turns from the supplicating voice his ear;
One starves in poverty; one is Amir
And drives his elephant in lordly state;
One lives in love; one girdled round with hate
Dwells ever in a bitter world of strife;
One in the moment of this earthly life
Is ruler, sitting on a regal seat;
One crawls a slave, obedient at his feet.

And Allah changes all as He desires,
He is an artist whom His art inspires:
This world the picture He is painting still.
But with his share of fate He gave man will
To fashion circumstance by its control,
To make a path of healing for his soul,
To act, to think, to feel aright until
He knows his will as one with Allah's will.

Shah Baz.

SHAH BAZ, the wondrous Bird, the Wanderer,
After his many travels far and wide
Returning, called a meeting of his friends
From hill, from sea, from lake, from countryside.

The gulls came from their nests among the cliffs,
The ducks and herons from the marshy lands,
The eagle from his eyrie in the sky,
The ostrich from the burning desert sands.

All gathered to receive him. Peacocks danced
To show their joy, and many a nightingale
Poured forth his welcome in harmonious verse,
While choirs of sky-larks sang their cheerful tale.

Then spoke Shah Baz and said: Far have I sped,
From pole to pole in anxious search I passed,
Till, worn by travel and by suffering,
The haven of my soul I won at last.

How can I tell the wonder of that land!
The sun is dim before its heavenly light,
And time with all its bondage is unknown,
No day is there, no dawn, no eve, no night.

The Sun, the Moon, and all the planets pale
Within the radiance of that light-filled sphere,
And earth and water all commingled are,
No hills, no separating seas appear.

Unchanging is the season and serene ;
  The happy airs that breathe of peace and home
Know neither cold nor storm, and over all
  There bends the kindly sky, an azure dome.

The raindrops are of pearl : fair are the hills,
  With gleams of gold their shining summits glow,
The foaming ocean is a sea of milk,
  The ever-brimming streams with honey flow.

And fair the lordly palaces arise,
  Carven by cunning skill, with many a gem
Encrusted and adorned, each haughty hall
  Wearing a diamond roof as diadem.

And there we strive with bitter chance no more ;
  For life flows onward in a tranquil stream,
And care and haunting sorrows fade and pass
  Like the remembrance of an evil dream.

Disease comes never there, and Death himself
  Dwells evermore without that happy gate,
No caste, nor creed, nor fortune can divide,
  For all are equal, free, and fortunate.

There heavenly Houris pour the Cousir's wine,
  That flows for all, and cheers and satisfies ;
And therefore am I sent to give the world
  The tidings—I, the Bird of Paradise.

And though I linger here to tell my tale,
  For that far country is my spirit fain ;
My wings are spread for flight ; I have declared
  My message ; and I seek my land again.

The birds pressed round; some ardently desired
  To seek that far-away and longed-for shore,
Some unbelievers scoffed, some doubted him,
  Some dreamed of it, desiring more and more.

Then said Shah Baz: Whose heart and will are firm,
  Whose patience is long suffering, whose desire
No disillusion nor despair can quench,
  Whose resolution will not faint nor tire,

O'er many lands and seas and oceans wide
  Through forests, through temptation's snares that lie
Thick on the path, his pilgrim soul shall fare
  To gain the land of truth and liberty.

And ponder, ere upon the difficult way
  You set your foot, what dangers may arise;
He who loves safe and idle ways of ease
  Shall never win the Land of Paradise.

And many flinched and failed. The chosen few
  Followed Shah Baz in hope; some strayed aside
And lost the path, some feared the endless sea,
  And tiring, fell upon the hills, and died.

But some attained, and after many days
  Their tears were done; their weariness, their sighs,
Were all forgotten as a dream at morn,
  Within the happy groves of Paradise.

Thus ALLAH sayeth to the hearts of men:
  My Messenger I have inspired and sent
To lead you to the Land beyond the World:
  O hear and heed, consider and repent!

The Lion's Cub.

A Lion old and wise
King of the Jungle, in the forest deep,
Saw, feeding 'neath the trees,
A flock of gentle, silly, helpless sheep.

And in their midst beheld
A lion's little cub with lambs at play,
Gambolling in the shade,
Drinking the stream, eating the grass as they.

He called, "O Lion, stay!
Have you forgot your parentage, my son?
Why bleat you like a sheep?
Why turn you like your stupid friends, to run?"

Then said the lion's cub,
"I am no lion, I am but a sheep;
Let me go with my flock
Among my own. I tremble and I weep."

"Blind art thou, O my child!"
The lion said, "but if thou follow me,
Down to the river-side
I will unseal thine eyes, so thou shalt see.

"I am the King of Beasts
Whom all obey, so with me must thou go."
"Alas," the cub replied,
"The sheep-fold and the sheep are all I know."

" Upon the water pure
Behold thy clear-reflected image shine,
Art thou indeed a sheep
Or is thy form a lordly one like mine ? "

Then from the youngling's eyes
The veil of ignorance was drawn aside
" I am of kingly blood,
I am a lion, Lord," he said with pride.

So man, awake and know !
Read in the holy pages of Korán
The words that Allah spoke :
" In mine own image have I moulded man."

Dialogue between Murshid and Mureed.

WHENCE have we come, O Murshid, whither pass we
  After this life, woven of joy and pain?
From out the life unconscious and immortal
  Our soul is drawn and must return again.

O tell me what is God, and what may Man be,
  And what within us is this life and breath,
What fate involved us in the web of being,
  And why comes suffering, and what is Death?

God is Eternal and is self-existent,
  Himself in earth and man He manifests,
He acts in all that lives and moves and suffers,
  And yet remote, withdrawn, aloof He rests.

When was this mighty Universe created,
  Shall it pursue its course, and be destroyed?
And how can man by seeking gain perfection,
  And Death, the Hunter of the Soul, avoid?

Again and yet again Creation's morning
  Has summoned up new wondrous worlds, and then
The night of dark Destruction has descended
  Dissolving them to Chaos once again.

But Man, self-mastering, can win perfection,
  Merging his puny self into the Whole,
The Self of God, that ocean-like surrounds him;
  Death holds his body, not his kingly soul.

And after death do we again awaken
In Heaven exulting, or despair in Hell?
These, child, are names and nothing, vain delusions,
The soul doth deathless, birthless, changeless, dwell,

Serene and ever-lasting, self-sufficient,
And all the earth's experience shall seem,
Toil being finished and desire transcended,
The fevered visions of a troubled dream.

The Dream of Life.

I HOLD that life is but a passing dream
  Out of the shifting mists of Maya made,
Our foolish hopes are children's fantasies,
  Out sorrows but the shadow of a shade.

And we, Earth's children, strive with eager hate
  And jealousy to snatch the passing joys
Of fame, and rank, and wealth, and power, and ease,
  As children quarrel over idle toys.

What is this life that surges, but the fall
  And rise of waves in an unquiet sea !
What is this worldly honour but a name
  To snare the feet of poor simplicity !

Master and servant, friend and foe alike,
  God for His lordly pleasure doth engage
As actors in the tragic Drama played
  In ever-changing scenes upon life's stage.

As shadows in the Theatre of Dreams
  Perform their part and pass into the night,
So Man in life's unending Masque appears
  And fades, to leave the curtain blank and white.

He travels on but knows not where he fares,
  Nor whence he comes, nor where the journey ends ;
He greets his fellow-travellers who pass
  Into the darkness, beckoning to their friends.

Enslaved by his insatiable needs
   Man toils to still their tyrannous demands,
Himself a serf, he strives in vain to rule,
   Life turns to dust and ashes in his hands.

* * * *

No pride of nationality is mine,
   Nor caste nor creed can tie me with its chain,
No narrow fatherland can bind my heart,
   For me the pride of birth and rank is vain.

No Heaven allures with unattained desire,
   No fair beloved is there for me to meet,
No Saviour offers cleansing for my sin,
   No God bends down my ransomed soul to greet.

No home have I, no friend, no name is mine,
   Nor man, nor God is kin unto my soul,
Over the Self, that formless, changeless dwells,
   No earthly limitations have control.

Nor birth nor death can touch my spirit more,
   Nor love nor hate can bring me peace nor strife,
The Self Within I have desired and found,
   And thus awakened from the Dream of Life.

Consciousness.

THOU one Eternal Infinite Consciousness,
Free from all name and form and change art Thou,
Free from all passing attributes ; in Thee
The rich and poor and good and evil meet :
Thy radiance is the Universal Soul,
Each human soul is but a ray of Thee :
Thou in the Universe art manifest,
And Thou Thyself art the Immortal Goal.
We are the rays of Thee, Eternal Sun,
And live and move in Thee. All evil is
But the illusion of our separateness.
Thou art Thyself our veritable life,
And manifestation does but clothe Thy Self
In souls and bodies and in hearts of men.
All great religions that the world hath known
Proclaim alike the knowledge of the Lord,
And Saints and Sages and the mystic souls
Who find the secret path, all seek for Thee.
Faiths and beliefs reveal our ignorance,
This Universe is but the play of God.
In all existence art Thou, One, Alone ;
But in thy different aspects we proclaim
Thy being as the Holy Trinity—
The Mother-spirit, Father, and the Son.
Again as Allah do we call on Thee,
The Merciful and the Compassionate.
Knower and Actor Thou of all our deeds,
Inspirer Thou of all we feel and do,

Watching our virtues and our failings both.
Master and Lord art Thou of Judgment Day,
Tenderly guiding Thy beloved ones
Lest from the path of virtue they should stray.

O God of man, and even God of Gods,
Eternal Holy Consciousness art Thou,
O shine within me that my very soul
May gleam with radiance it hath caught from Thee!

Death.

WITHIN my slumber deep
Turning unquietly from side to side I stirred;
Death rocked me saying: Night is not yet o'er,
So slumber on!—I heard his gentle word.

Languidly I awake,
And watch Life in its sequence passing on,
But o'er me sleep hangs like a heavy cloud,
Death says: Sleep still—it is not yet the dawn.

Appendix I

THE AIMS OF THE SUFI MOVEMENT

The Movement is based upon the Sufi Message brought to the Western world by Hazrat Inayat Khan in 1910.

In his studies as an initiate in one of the ancient Sufi orders, Inayat Khan recognised the basic love and wisdom through which humanity may realize the purpose of life. He saw these two principles as enshrined in the ideals of all religions. He held that by honouring all, and respecting their differences, a basis for mutual understanding could be reached which would not be possible by seeking to convert one to the views of another.

In pursuance of his vision he came to the West, and taught in Europe and America until 1926 when, shortly before his passing, he returned to India. He called his teaching the Sufi Message and to propagate it he founded a body called the International Sufi Movement. In the constitution are enshrined the following Sufi Thoughts:

1. There is one God, the Eternal, the Only Being; none else exists save He.
2. There is one Master, the Guiding Spirit of all souls, who constantly leads his followers towards the light.
3. There is one Holy Book, the sacred manuscript of nature, the only scripture which can enlighten the reader.
4. There is one Religion, the unswerving progress in the right direction towards the ideal, which fulfils the life's purpose of every soul.
5. There is one Law, the Law of Reciprocity, which can be observed by a selfless conscience together with a sense of awakened justice.
6. There is one Brotherhood, the human brotherhood, which unites the children of earth indiscriminately in the fatherhood of God.
7. There is one Moral Principle, the love which springs forth from self-denial, and blooms in deeds of beneficence.
8. There is one Object of Praise, the beauty which uplifts the heart of its worshipper through all aspects from the seen to the unseen.
9. There is one Truth, the true knowledge of our being within and without which is the essence of all wisdom.

10. There is one Path, the annihilation of the false ego in the real, which raises the mortal to immortality and in which resides all perfection.

The Movement has the following Objects:

1. To realize and spread the knowledge of unity, the religion of love and wisdom, so that the bias of faiths and beliefs may of itself fall away, the human heart may overflow with love, and all hatred caused by distinctions and differences may be rooted out.
2. To discover the light and power latent in man, the secret of all religion, the power of mysticism, and the essence of philosophy, without interfering with customs or belief.
3. To help to bring the world's two opposite poles, East and West, closer together by the interchange of thought and ideals, that the Universal Brotherhood may form of itself, and man may meet with man beyond the narrow national and racial boundaries.

Regarding the aims of the Movement, we quote as follows from the words of Inayat Khan:

"The purpose of the Sufi Movement is to work towards unity. Its main object is to bring humanity, divided as it is into so many different sections, closer together in the deeper understanding of life. It is a preparation for a world service, chiefly in three ways. One way is the philosophical understanding of life; another is bringing about brotherhood among races, nations, and creeds; and the third way is the meeting of the world's greatest need, which is the religion of the day. Its work is to bring to the world that natural religion which has always been the religion of humanity: to respect one another's belief, scripture, and teacher. The Sufi message is the echo of the same divine message which has always come and will always come to enlighten humanity. It is not a new religion; it is the same message which is being given to humanity. It is the continuation of the same ancient religion which has always existed and will always exist, a religion which belongs to all teachers and all the scriptures.

"Sufism in itself is not a religion nor even a cult with a distinct or definite doctrine. No better explanation of Sufism can be given than by saying that any person who has a knowledge of both outer and inner life is a Sufi. Thus there has never at any period of the world's history been a founder of Sufism, yet Sufism has existed at all times.

"The present-day Sufi Movement is a movement of members of different nations and races united together in the ideal of wisdom; they believe that wisdom does not belong to any particular religion or race, but to the human race as a whole. It is a divine property which mankind has inherited; and it is in this realization that the Sufis, in spite of belonging to different nationalities, races, beliefs, and faiths, still unite and work for humanity in the ideal of wisdom.

"The Sufi message warns humanity to get to know life better and to achieve freedom in life; it warns man to accomplish what he considers good, just, and desirable; it warns him before every action to note its consequences by studying the situation, his own attitude, and the method he should adopt.

"Sufism not only guides those who are religious, mystical, or visionary, but the Sufi message gives to the world the religion of the day: and that is to make one's life a religion, to turn one's occupation or profession into a religion, to make one's ideal a religious ideal. The object of Sufism is the uniting of life and religion, which so far seem to have been kept apart. When a man goes to church once a week, and devotes all the other days of the week to his business, how can he benefit by religion? Therefore, the teaching of Sufism is to transform everyday life into a religion, so that every action may bear some spiritual fruit.

"The method of world reform which various institutions have adopted today is not the method of the Sufi Movement. Sufis believe that if evil is contagious, goodness must be even more so. The depth of every soul is good; every soul is searching for good, and by the effort of individuals who wish to do good in the world much can be done, even more than a materialistic institution can achieve. No doubt for the general good there are political and commercial problems to be solved; but that must not debar individuals from progress, for it is the individual progress through the spiritual path which alone can bring about the desired condition in the world.

"The Sufi message is not for a particular race, nation, or church. It is a call to unite in wisdom. The Sufi Movement is a group of people belonging to different religions, who have not left their religions but who have learned to understand them better, and their love is the love for God and humanity instead of for a particular section of it. The principal work that the Sufi Movement has to accomplish is to bring about a better understanding between East and West, and between the nations and races of his world. And the note that the sufi message is striking at the present time is the note which sounds the divinity of the human soul. If there is any moral principle that the Sufi Movement brings, it is this: that the whole of humanity is like one body, and any organ of that body which is hurt or troubled can indirectly cause damage to the whole body. And as the health of the whole body depends upon the health of each part, so the health of the whole of humanity depends upon the health of every nation. Besides, to those who are awakening and feel that now is the moment to learn more of the deeper side of life, of truth, the Sufi Movement extends a helping hand without asking to what religion, sect, or dogma they belong. The knowledge of the Sufi is helpful to every person, not only in living his life rightly but in regard to his own religion. The Sufi Movement does not call a man away from his belief or chruch: it calls him to live it. In short, it is a movement intended by God to unite humanity in brotherhood and in wisdom."

From *The Sufi Message of Hazrat Inayat Khan,* Volume IX

Those desiring particulars regarding the activities in all countries of the Sufi Movement founded by Hazrat Inayat Khan should apply to the International Headquarters of the Movement as follows:

(for activities in India)
Sufi Movement India,
Dargah Hzt. Inayat Khan
129, Basti Hzt. Nizamuddin
New Delhi 110 013

(for activities outside India)
General Secretariat,
Sufi Movement,
Anna Paulownastraat 78
2518 BJ The Hague
Holland

GLOSSARY.

Akbar ... ... Mogul Emperor of India.
Allah-ho-Akbar ... God is great.
Amir ... ... rich.
Badshahi ... ... royal.
Bostan ... ... place of fragrance.
Cousir ... ... stream of heavenly wine.
Deepak Râg ... musical theme of fire.
Dozakh ... ... purgatory.
Gulistan ... ... place of roses.
Houris ... ... nymphs of Heaven.
Huzoor ... ... the presence (term of respect).
Inayat ... ... favour.
Islam ... ... Belief in Allah alone.
Jennat ... ... Heaven.
Kaaba ... ... central shrine at Mecca.
Kafir ... ... unbeliever.
Kismet ... ... fate.
Koran ... ... sacred Book of Islam.
Kussam ... ... fate-maker.
Malhar Râg ... musical theme of water.
Malkous Râg ... musical theme of ecstasy.
Maya ... ... illusion.
Muslim ... ... one believing in Allah alone.
Mureed ... ... disciple.
Murshid ... ... spiritual teacher.
Nargis ... ... narcissus.
Najat ... ... salvation.
Satan (*Shaitan*) ... principle of Evil.
Pir ... ... revered one.
Rahman ... ... principle of Good.
Rezk ... ... food.
Ruzak ... ... the sustaining (food-giving) aspect of Allah.
Saki ... ... wine-giver.
Saki-i-Alishan ... exalted wine-giver.
Shah Baz ... ... bird of Paradise.
Sura ... ... sentence or verse.
Tansen ... ... a great Indian singer.
Vina ... ... stringed musical instrument played with the fingers.